Samuel French Acting Edition

The Haggadah

Adapted and Composed by
Elizabeth Swados

English text by Elie Wiesel

I0589027

‖ SAMUEL FRENCH ‖

SAMUELFRENCH.COM   SAMUELFRENCH.CO.UK

Copyright © 1982 by Elizabeth Swados
"God of Mercy" lyric translated from the Yiddish of Kadia Molodowsky
by Pearl Lang. Used by Permission.
All Rights Reserved
"Pesach Has Come" adapted from "In Varshever Ghetto Iz Itst Khoydesh
Nisn" by Binem Heller

THE HAGGADAH is fully protected under the copyright laws of the
United States of America, the British Commonwealth, including Canada,
and all other countries of the Copyright Union. All rights, including professional and amateur stage productions, recitation, lecturing, public
reading, motion picture, radio broadcasting, television and the rights of
translation into foreign languages are strictly reserved.

ISBN 978-0-573-68106-6

www.SamuelFrench.com
www.SamuelFrench.co.uk

FOR PRODUCTION ENQUIRIES

UNITED STATES AND CANADA
Info@SamuelFrench.com
1-866-598-8449

UNITED KINGDOM AND EUROPE
Plays@SamuelFrench.co.uk
020-7255-4302

Each title is subject to availability from Samuel French, depending
upon country of performance. Please be aware that THE HAGGADAH
may not be licensed by Samuel French in your territory. Professional
and amateur producers should contact the nearest Samuel French
office or licensing partner to verify availability.

CAUTION: Professional and amateur producers are hereby warned that
THE HAGGADAH is subject to a licensing fee. Publication of this play(s)
does not imply availability for performance. Both amateurs and profes-
sionals considering a production are strongly advised to apply to Samuel
French before starting rehearsals, advertising, or booking a theatre. A
licensing fee must be paid whether the title(s) is presented for charity or
gain and whether or not admission is charged. Professional/Stock licensing fees are quoted upon application to Samuel French.

No one shall make any changes in this title(s) for the purpose of
production. No part of this book may be reproduced, stored in a retrieval
system, or transmitted in any form, by any means, now known or yet to
be invented, including mechanical, electronic, photocopying, recording,
videotaping, or otherwise, without the prior written permission of the
publisher. No one shall upload this title(s), or part of this title(s), to any
social media websites.

Please refer to page 70 for further copyright information.

A New York Shakespeare Festival Production

Joseph Papp

PRESENTS

THE HAGGADAH

A Passover Cantata

BY
Elizabeth Swados

ADAPTED AND DIRECTED BY
The Composer

NARRATION ADAPTED FROM TEXTS BY
Elie Wiesel

SCENERY, COSTUMES, PUPPETRY AND MASKS BY
Julie Taymor

LIGHTING BY
Arden Fingerhut

WITH

Richard Allen   Anthony B. Asbury   Shami Chaikin   Craig Chang

Victor Cook   Sheila Dabney   Jossie de Guzman

Michael Edward-Stevens   Onni Johnson   Sally Kate   Esther Levy

Larry Marshall   Steven Memel   Martin Robinson

David Schechter   Peter Schlosser   Zvee Scooler

Ira Siff   Louise Smith   Kerry Stubbs

MUSICIANS
Carolyn Dutton   Judith Fleisher   Leopoldo F. Fleming
Robert J. Magnuson   David Sawyer

The Event   The Cast

*Arrangements and final chorale by Carolyn Dutton

THE HAGGADAH is performed without an intermission.

Production Supervisor for the New York Shakespeare Festival:
Jason Steven Cohen

The Haggadah is based on *Moses: Portrait of a Leader* from
Messenger of God: Biblical Portraits by Elie Wiesel, and por-
tions of The Haggadah, the Old Testament and the poetry of
Gabriela Mistral, Kadia Molodowsky and Elie Wiesel. All Elie
Wiesel material translated by Marian Wiesel.

By the Waters of Babylon and *Hoshiyanaw* are derived from
traditional melodies.

The seder is a family service which takes place around a dinner
table. Friends (especially non-Jewish friends) are invited. The
table is set with items that symbolize various aspects of the Jews'
slavery and subsequent exodus from Egypt. Bitter herbs symbolize the bitterness of slavery; salt water, the tears of slavery. A
mixture of apples and matzoh make the *moror*—the mortar
which built the pyramids. There are many symbols and throughout the evening they are presented, tasted and discussed so that,
in effect, the family may live through their ancestors' past. The
text for the seder is a book called *The Haggadah*, which gives the
prayers, songs and discussion which take the family through the
evening. Many versions of the book exist, from the traditional
Hebrew to more ecumenical versions which incorporate the poetry and song of other cultures. Through the observance of Passover, the Jewish people recall their past as slaves in Egypt and
are reminded, every year, that one must not rest until all men are
free. The concept of continuity is essential to the celebration of
this holiday. One generation passes ideas to the next through
questions, games, fables and songs—rituals shared equally
by all.

THE HAGGADAH was first presented by Joseph Papp at the New York Shakespeare Festival, the Public/Luesther Hall in New York City in the Spring 1980, with the following cast:

Roger Babb
Suzanne Baxtresser
Shami Chaikin
Craig Chang
Victor Cook
Keith David
Patrick Jude
Aisha Kahlil
Esther Levy
John S. Lewandowski
Martha Plimpton
Martin Robinson
Wes Sanders
David Schechter
Kate Schmitt
Zvee Scooler
Ira Siff
Kerry Stubbs
Deborah Anne Wise

Musicians:
Carolyn Dutton
Judith Fleisher
Leopoldo F. Fleming
Vincent Penella
David W. Sawyer

This version of THE HAGGADAH was performed during Spring 1981 at the New York Shakespeare Festival, Public Theatre/ Luesther Hall, with the following cast:

Richard Allen	Tenor
Anthony B. Asbury	Tenor
Shami Chaikin	Alto
Craig Chang	Boy Soprano
Victor Cook	Boy Soprano
Sheila Dabney	Alto
Jossie de Guzman	Soprano
Michael Edward-Stevens	Bass/Baritone
Onni Johnson	Soprano/Alto
Sally Kate	Soprano
Esther Levy	Alto
Larry Marshall	Tenor
Steven Memel	Baritone
Martin Robinson	Bass/Baritone
David Schechter	Baritone
Peter Schlosser	Bass/Baritone
Zvee Scooler	Narrator
Ira Siff	Baritone/Tenor
Louise Smith	Soprano
Kerry Stubbs	Boy Soprano

Musicians:

Carolyn Dutton	Violin
Judith Fleisher	Piano
Leopoldo F. Fleming	Percussion
Robert J. Magnuson	Flute/Clarinet
David W. Sawyer	Percussion

Instruments used:

Piano/Celeste/Organ
Violin
Flute
Clarinet
Accordian
Zither
Percussion: Trap Set, Tom Toms, Timpani, Gongs (A & D), Tam Tam, Bass Drum, Cymbals (bow), Conch Shell, Drum Sticks, Soft Mallets, Crotales, Tambourine, Agogo Bell, Cow Bell, Moroccan Drum, Plexiglass Sheets, Long Pipes.

THE HAGGADAH is a continuous piece of music. In almost all instances (except where indicated), one section flows immediately into the next. In other words, the final beat of the last measure of one song is followed immediately by the first beat of the first measure in the next song. This is indicated in the score by the words "Immediate Segue" at the end of each selection. If there is a tempo change it is so indicated. If no tempo change is noted, the song maintains the same tempo as the previous number.

All of the Hebrew lyrics in this score are written in English phoenetically. Because it is difficult to convey many of the inflections and nuances in the Hebrew language in this manner, it is recommended that performers consult with someone conversant in the language for exact pronunciations.

This script indicates the way in which the production was directed by Ms. Swados who chose to utilize the designs of Julie Taymor and the specific qualifications of Luesther Hall at the New York Shakespeare Festival. It is by no means the only way to visualize the event, although it has proved successful. If directors do not have access to a room with two sides or designers who make shadow puppets, the composer suggests listening to the oratorio and interpreting it in new ways. In other words, groups should not be discouraged from performing THE HAGGADAH if their space and budget limitations cannot fulfill the intent of the stage directions.

The Haggadah

THE FOUR QUESTIONS

(CRAIG *and* SALLY *enter from opposite sides at East End of hall during celeste introduction. They meet in front of pyramid. While reciting the four questions, they walk slowly from East end of space to West end, stop on first level of mountain and turn to face East end.*)

CRAIG. (*Sung.*)
MA NISH TA NAH HA LAI
LAH HAZEH
MIKOL HA LAY LOS?
SHE B'CHOL HA LAY LOS
ANU
OCHLEEN CH MAYTZ U
MATZAH, HA
LAI LAH HA ZEH KULO
MATZAH?

SHE B'CHOL HA LAY LOS
ANU
OCHLEEN SH'AR Y'RA
KOS HA LAI
LAH HAZEH MOROR.

SHE B'CHOL HA LAY LOS
AYN ANU
MAT BEE LEEN A FEE LOO
PA AM
ECHAS HA LAI LAH
HAZEH SH'TAY
PE'HA MEEM?

SHE B'CHOL HA LAY LOS
ANU OCHLEEN
BAYN YOSH VEEN U
VAYN M'SU BEEN.
HA LAI LAH HAZEH U
VAYNO
M'SU BEEN.

SALLY. (*Spoken.*)
Why is this night different from
all other nights?
On all other nights we eat
leavened or unleavened bread.
Why on this night do we eat only
matzah, the unleavened bread?

On all other nights we eat all kinds of herbs. Why on this night
do we eat especially moror, the bitter herb?

On all other nights we do not dip
herbs even once. Why on this night do we dip twice, first the green in salt water and then the bitter herb into charoses?

On all other nights we may eat at the table either sitting up erect or reclining. Why on this night do we recline?

9

PRELUDE (*Flute Underscore.*)

ZVEE. (*Enters from Northeast, walks to front of pyramid and reads from book.*)
The Baal Shem Tov, founder of Hassidism, used to go to a certain place in the woods and light a fire and pray when he was faced with an especially difficult task and it was done.

His successor followed his example and went to the same place but said, "The fire we can no longer light, but we can still say the prayer." And what he asked was done too.

Another generation passed, and Rabbi Moshe Leib of Sassov went to the woods and said, "The fire we can no longer light, the prayer we no longer know. All we know is the place in the woods, and that will have to be enough." And it was enough.

In the fourth generation, Rabbi Israel of Rishin stayed at home and said, "The fire we can no longer light, the prayer we no longer know, nor do we know the place. All we can do is tell the story."

And that, too, proved sufficient.

(ZVEE *exits* N.E.)

PESACH HAS COME TO THE GHETTO

(COMPANY *enters from all four corners and sits on floor in two lines along both sides of space.*)

ONNI. (*Moves around inside circle singing to* COMPANY *and audience.*)
PESACH HAS COME TO THE GHETTO AGAIN.
THE WINE HAS NO GRAPE, THE MATZAH NO GRAIN,
BUT THE PEOPLE ANEW SING THE WONDERS OF OLD.
THE FLIGHT FROM THE PHARAOHS, SO OFTEN RETOLD.
HOW ANCIENT THE STORY, HOW OLD THE REFRAIN!

THE WINDOWS ARE SHUTTERED.
THE DOORS ARE CONCEALED.

THE SEDER GOES ON
AND FICTION AND FACT ARE CONFUSED INTO ONE.
WHICH IS MYTH?
WHICH IS REAL?

"COME ALL WHO ARE HUNGRY!"
INVITES THE HAGGADAH.
THE HELPLESS, THE AGED,
LIE STARVING IN FEAR.
"COME ALL WHO ARE HUNGRY!"
AND CHILDREN SLEEP, FAMISHED.
"COME ALL WHO ARE HUNGRY!"
AND TABLES ARE BARE.

    JOSSIE. (*Stands and crosses to center of circle. Moves around inside circle as she sings.*)
PESACH HAS COME TO THE GHETTO AGAIN.
THE WINE HAS NO GRAPE, THE MATZAH NO GRAIN,
BUT THE PEOPLE ANEW SING THE WONDERS OF OLD.
THE FLIGHT FROM THE PHARAOHS, SO OFTEN
RETOLD.
HOW ANCIENT THE STORY, HOW OLD THE REFRAIN!

BUT THESE ARE THE SHARDS,
THE SHATTERED REMAINS
OF THE "SIXTY TEN-THOUSANDS"
WHOM MOSES LED OUT OF THEIR BONDAGE
DRIVEN TO GHETTOS AGAIN . . .
WHERE DYING'S PERMITTED
BUT PROTEST IS NOT.

    COMPANY.
"COME ALL WHO ARE HUNGRY!"
INVITES THE HAGGADAH.
THE HELPLESS, THE AGED,
LIE STARVING IN FEAR.
"COME ALL WHO ARE HUNGRY!"
AND CHILDREN SLEEP, FAMISHED.
"COME ALL WHO ARE HUNGRY!"
AND TABLES ARE BARE.

    ONNI & JOSSIE.
PESACH HAS COME TO THE GHETTO AGAIN.
THE LORE-LADEN WORDS OF THE SEDER ARE SAID,
AND THE CUP OF THE PROPHET ELIJAH AWAITS,

BUT THE ANGEL OF DEATH HAS INTRUDED, INSTEAD.
    JOSSIE.
WHO SHALL LIVE,
    JOSSIE & ONNI.
WHO SHALL DIE
    COMPANY.
WHO SHALL LIVE
WHO SHALL DIE
    JOSSIE & ONNI. (*Slap floor with hands.*)
THIS PASSOVER NIGHT.
    COMPANY. (*Stands and turns to face audience.*)
"COME ALL WHO ARE HUNGRY!"
INVITES THE HAGGADAH.
THE HELPLESS, THE AGED,
LIE STARVING IN FEAR.
"COME ALL WHO ARE HUNGRY!"
AND CHILDREN SLEEP, FAMISHED.
"COME ALL WHO ARE HUNGRY!"
    JOSSIE & ONNI.
AND TABLES ARE BARE.

SHIR HA SHI RIM

(*During song,* COMPANY *stands facing audience, arms at sides.*
    MICHAEL *picks up* CRAIG *and holds him over his head, starts
    crossing around to walk to pyramid.* COMPANY *follows.*
    MARTIN, DAVID, ANTHONY, LOUISE *exit to pyramid. As*
    MICHAEL/CRAIG *pass* COMPANY *they turn and face and walk
    East.*)

    COMPANY.
SHIR HA SHI RIM
A SHER LI SH'LO MOH
YI SHA KE NI
MI NE SHI KOT
PI HU KI TO VIM
DO DE CHA MI YA YIN
LE RE ACH SHE MA NE CHA TO VIM
SHE MEN TU RAK SHE ME CHA
AL KEN A LA MOT A HE VU CHA
SHIR HA SHI RIM

A SHER LI SH'LO MOH
SHIR HA SHI RIM
A SHER LI SH'LO MOH

(MICHAEL *lifts* CRAIG *onto pyramid.* LOUISE *in mask is there to receive him as mother.*)

JOSSIE. (LOUISE *holds* CRAIG *on pyramid.* MARTIN, DAVID *and* ANTHONY, *in masks on pyramid, watch them.*)
AVODIM HAYINU
AVODIM HAYINU
COMPANY. (*Chant.* COMPANY *turns to face West End. They chant and stamp one foot in rhythm, looking down.* MARTIN, ANTHONY *and* DAVID *take* CRAIG/MOSES *from* LOUISE *and throw him up and down in rhythm to chant.*)
AVODIM HAYINU
EVERY SON THAT IS BORN TO
THE HEBREWS
AVODIM HAYINU
YOU SHALL CAST
INTO THE NILE
AVODIM HAYINU
EVERY SON THAT IS BORN
TO THE HEBREWS
AVODIM HAYINU
YOU SHALL CAST
INTO THE NILE
COMPANY. (MARTIN, ANTHONY *and* DAVID *place* CRAIG *in position to fall off pyramid.*)
AVODIM . . .

(CRAIG *falls into men's arms. They lift* CRAIG *up on* MICHAEL'S *shoulders.*)

STEVE. (ALL *indicate* CRAIG *with one arm.*)
Moses, the most solitary and most
powerful hero in Biblical history.

(*During piano intro,* ALL *cross into floor positions and sit.* MICHAEL *carries* CRAIG *to center.* ONNI *stands next to* CRAIG.)

NARRATION 1

ONNI. (*Hands on* CRAIG'S *shoulders.*)
HIS LIFE BEGAN WITH TEARS,
HIS OWN.
BATYA, THE PHARAOH'S DAUGHTER,
NOTICED A BASKET FLOATING DOWN THE NILE
AND DISCOVERED IN IT A JEWISH INFANT
SHE KNEW IT WAS JEWISH BECAUSE IT CRIED
NOT LIKE AN INFANT BUT LIKE AN ADULT,
LIKE A COMMUNITY OF ADULTS
    COMPANY. (*Stand.*)
HIS ENTIRE PEOPLE WAS CRYING IN HIM

(ALL *turn out to audience, stamp foot — strong step side together,
    right then left.*)

    CHORUS.
AH AH AH AH AH AH AH
    IRA/ONNI.
MOSHE
    CHORUS.
AH AH AH AH AH AH AH
    IRA/ONNI.
WERE IT NOT FOR HIM
    CHORUS.
AH AH AH AH AH AH AH
    IRA/ONNI.
ISRAEL WOULD HAVE REMAINED
    CHORUS.
AH AH AH AH AH AH AH
    IRA/ONNI
A TRIBE OF SLAVES

(ALL *sit but* LARRY.)

    LARRY.
LEGEND TELLS US THAT MOSES DID NOT
WISH TO CRY.
    CHORUS.
AH AH AH AH
    LARRY.
ON THE CONTRARY HE TRIED TO HOLD BACK

HIS TEARS.
CHORUS.
AH AH AH AH
LARRY.
TO REMAIN CALM AND SILENT THOUGH HE
WAS AFRAID.

(LARRY *sits and* SHAMI *stands.*)

SHAMI.
AT THREE YEARS OF AGE
HE DISPLAYED THE GIFTS OF A HEALER
AND OF A PROPHET
COMPANY. (*Hold up right hands indicating* CRAIG.)
AND OF A PROPHET, AND OF A PROPHET.
DAVID. (*Standing, turning and crossing to* CRAIG.)
LAI LAI LAI LAI
LAI LAI LAI LAI
LAI
WE ARE TOLD NOTHING ABOUT HIS ADOLESCENCE.
WE ARE ONLY TOLD THAT ONE DAY
HE GREW UP AND WENT OUT TO SEE HIS BRETHREN.
COMPANY. (*Stands. Hit chests and gesture out.*)
ET ECHAV.
DAVID.
THE GERER REBBE INTERPRETS THIS AS MEANING:
MOSES' GREATNESS WAS THAT HE WENT OUT TO
JOIN HIS PEOPLE
COMPANY.
VAYIGDAL MOSHE VAYETZE EL ECHAV.
VAYIGDAL MOSHE VAYETZE EL ECHAV.
VAYIGDAL MOSHE VAYETZE EL ECHAV.

(SHEILA, RICHARD, MARTIN, LOUISE, ANTHONY *and* DAVID *cross
to pyramid and put on masks and exit to get into bubus and
get pyramids.* COMPANY *sits.*)

SLAVE CHANT

ESTHER. (*Enters from West End and walks to second step of
mountain.*)
AVADIM HAYINU L'PHARAOH B'MITZRAYIM
ZVEE. (*Spoken.*)

We were slaves to Pharaoh in Egypt.
ESTHER. (*Crossing off mountain.*)
AVODIM HAYINU L'PHARAOH
B'MITZRAYIM
ZVEE. (*Spoken.*)
We were slaves to Pharaoh in Egypt.
ESTHER.
AVODIM HAYINU L'PHARAOH
B'MITZRAYIM.

(*During the Slave Chant,* ESTHER *crosses to the East End,* RICHARD *enters with small pyramid, then the big pyramid carried by* DAVID, ANTHONY *and* MARTIN, *then the medium pyramid carried by* SHEILA *and* LOUISE. CRAIG *stands center and watches the pyramids pass.*)

COMPANY.	ESTHER. (*Sung 3 times.*)
AH AH AH AH AH AH AH AH	VAYAR ISH MITZRI
AH AH AH AH AH AH AH AH	MAH KEH ISH IVRI
AH AH AH AH AH AH AH AH	VAYEEFEN KOH VEH
AH AH AH AH AH AH AH AH	CHOL
	VAYAR KAIN ISH
AH AH AH AH AH AH AH AH	
AH AH AH AH AH AH AH AH	VAYEH CHASH EL
	HAMITZRI
AH AH AH AH AH AH AH AH	V'YAT MENEH HU
AH AH AH AH AH AH AH AH	RACHOL
AH AH AH AH AH AH AH AH	VAYEH CHASH EL
AH AH AH AH AH AH AH AH	HAMITZRI
	V'YAT MENEH HU
AH AH AH AH AH AH AH AH	RACHOL
AH AH AH AH AH AH AH AH	
AH AH AH AH AH AH AH AH	
AH AH AH AH AH AH AH AH	
AH AH AH AH AH AH AH AH	
AH AH AH AH AH AH AH AH	

(*Pyramid carriers stop and wait. On 4th Timpani beat, pyramid holders stamp feet.* VICTOR, ONNI *and* JOSSIE *roll under pyramids which are lowered on top of them. They scream with arms pushing out to sides.* MICHAEL *stands and makes whipping motions.*)

SHAMI.
ADOSHEM ADOSHEM LAWMAW HAREOHSAW
LAWOHM HAZEH, ADOSHEM ADOSHEM
ONNI, JOSSIE, VICTOR. (*As pyramids lower.*)
AH . . .
SHAMI. (*Whisper.*)
Adoshem
CRAIG. (*Whisper.*)
Adoshem
SHAMI.
Lawmaw
CRAIG.
Lawmaw
SHAMI.
Hareohsaw
CRAIG.
Hareohsaw
SHAMI.
Lawohm
CRAIG.
Lawohm
SHAMI.
Hazeh
CRAIG.
Hazeh
COMPANY. (*Whisper.*)
Oh God, why has thou done evil to this people?
COMPANY. (*Turn out and sing in unison. Pyramids lifted quickly.* CRAIG *walks and looks at each pyramid; as he does, pyramid holders strike pose.*)
MOSES SAW STRONG MEN CARRYING LIGHT BURDENS.
MOSES SAW WEAK MEN STRAINING UNDER HEAVY LOADS.
MOSES SAW OLD MEN PERFORMING THE TASKS OF YOUNG MEN.
MOSES SAW YOUNG MEN DOING WORK SUITED FOR OLD MEN.

(*Pyramids are carried off.*)

VAYIGDAL MOSHE VAYETZE EL ECHAV.
VAYIGDAL MOSHE VAYETZE EL ECHAV.
VAYIGDAL MOSHE VAYETZE EL ECHAV.

GOD OF FAITHFUL

(*During poem,* RICHARD, LOUISE, SHEILA, DAVID, ANTHONY, MARTIN *and* ESTHER *put on masks and get into Babylon positions on moat.*)

SHAMI.
God faithful
To a faithful people,
God of cruelty,
God of silence,
Morning sun,
Sun of fear,
You awaken the beast and you kill man —
Heavenly silence, human silence,
You oppress the soul crying its hunger —
Sky in flames, sky of night:
A cry goes up,
But who will hear?

SHAMI, LARRY, MICHAEL & STEVE. (*Men stand up and walk to center.* SHAMI *sits.*)
Who will hear and who will listen?
Who will understand,
Who will repeat?

BY THE WATERS OF BABYLON

(*Throughout song, slaves on moats pantomime pulling ropes in slow, stylized movements. In slow motion,* MARTIN *beats* ANTHONY *on top of pyramid.*)

LARRY, STEVE & MICHAEL. (*Stand one behind the other facing pyramids.*)
BY THE WATERS OF BABYLON,
THERE WE SAT DOWN AND WEPT,
THERE WE SAT DOWN AND WEPT,
WHEN WE REMEMBERED ZION.

BY THE WATERS OF BABYLON,
THERE WE SAT DOWN AND WEPT,

THERE WE SAT DOWN AND WEPT,
WHEN WE REMEMBERED ZION.

ON THE WILLOWS THERE
WE HUNG UP OUR LYRES.
FOR THERE OUR CAPTORS
REQUIRED OF US SONGS,
AND OUR TORMENTORS MIRTH,
SAYING:
SING US ONE OF THOSE SONGS OF ZION.
SING US ONE OF THOSE SONGS OF ZION.
SING US ONE OF THOSE SONGS OF ZION.
SING US ONE OF THOSE SONGS OF ZION.

(*Slaves take off masks and sing holding masks up and in front, alternating sides.*)

COMPANY. (*Stands.*)
HOW SHALL WE SING THE LORD'S SONG
IN A FOREIGN LAND?
HOW SHALL WE SING THE LORD'S SONG
IN A FOREIGN LAND?
HOW SHALL WE SING THE LORD'S SONG
IN A FOREIGN LAND?
HOW SHALL WE SING THE LORD'S SONG
IN A FOREIGN LAND?

AH   AH
AH   AH
AH   AH
AH
MICHAEL. (*Lifts* CRAIG *up and carries him to pyramid.* CRAIG *swings fist slowly 4 times at* MARTIN *who staggers at each blow (Pa, Pa, Pa, Pa,) and then falls.*)
AH . . . PA PA PA PA.

NARRATION 2

(*During piano intro,* MICHAEL *carries* CRAIG *back to center of hall and* JOSSIE *crosses to him.* COMPANY *on either side of hall kneels. Pyramid people remain at moats with masks.*)

JOSSIE.
ONE DAY WHEN HE SAW AN EGYPTIAN

OVERSEER TORTURING A SLAVE
HE THREW HIMSELF ON THE MAN AND KILLED HIM.
HE WANTED TO UNDERSTAND, TO HELP
TO UNDERSTAND IN ORDER TO BE ABLE TO HELP.
ONE DAY HE SAW TWO JEWS QUARRELING.
WHEN ONE BEGAN TO STRIKE THE OTHER,
HE INTERVENED.

CRAIG. (*Spoken in rhythm.* COMPANY *turns away from* CRAIG.)
Rasha, you wicked man,
Why are you striking your brother?

CHORUS. (*Group on floor crosses crouched low around* CRAIG *accusingly.*)
IN TRUTH IT HARDLY SEEMS TO HAVE BEEN
HIS BUSINESS.

WHY SHOULD AN EGYPTIAN PRINCE
CARE IF TWO JEWISH SLAVES
FELT LIKE HAVING A FIGHT?

CRAIG.
BUT HE ALREADY FELT COMMITTED AS A JEW
AND PEOPLE WERE BEGINNING TO TAKE NOTICE.

PYRAMID PEOPLE. (*Spoken; pointing at* CRAIG.)
Ha leh hargani a taw ohmer
A tah a tah asher ha rah ta etah mitzri

CHORUS. (*Spoken.*)
Spare us your sermons;
Are you planning to kill us too?

(CHORUS *walks away from* CRAIG *rejecting him.* ALL *turn away.*)

CRAIG. (*Stands in center and slowly turns.*)
DENOUNCED, BETRAYED, MOSES HAD TO FLEE.
IT WAS NOT EASY FOR A YOUNG MAN
USED TO A PRINCELY LIFE
AND THE FRIENDSHIP OF THE GREAT
TO BECOME A HELPLESS FUGITIVE OVERNIGHT.

LARRY. (*Stands.*)
WHEN HE ACCEPTED HIS NEW ALLEGIANCE,
MOSES BECAME A STRANGER
IN MORE WAYS THAN ONE.

PYRAMID PEOPLE. (*Turn to* CRAIG.)
A STRANGER TO THE EGYPTIAN PEOPLE,

CHORUS. (*On floor, turns in.*)
TO THE JEWISH PEOPLE

CRAIG. (*Chorus sits.*)
AND TO HIMSELF.
SHAMI. (*Stands and walks to West End of hall.* CHILDREN *cross onto mountain. Boys into place.* SALLY *goes for bubu on top of mountain.*)
AFTER MANY ADVENTURES
THE FUGITIVE ARRIVED IN THE LAND OF MIDIAN,
WHERE HE SETTLED,
HAVING FOUND FOOD AND SHELTER
AND WORK AS A SHEPHERD.

SHEPHERD SONG

(*As they sing,* SALLY *hands folded cloth symbolizing sheep to* KERRY *and* VICTOR.)

PYRAMID PEOPLE.
ONE DAY HE SAW A SHEEP LEAVE THE FLOCK;
HE PURSUED IT
UNTIL HE FOUND IT DRINKING FROM A STREAM.
AND MOSES SAID SOFTLY:
CHILDREN. (SALLY, VICTOR, KERRY *move feet side to side to beat.*)
I DIDN'T KNOW YOU WERE THIRSTY.
YOU MUST BE VERY TIRED AFTER RUNNING SO FAR;
YOU DON'T HAVE THE STRENGTH TO GO BACK.
CHILDREN & WOMEN.
I DIDN'T KNOW YOU WERE THIRSTY.
YOU MUST BE VERY TIRED AFTER RUNNING SO FAR.
YOU DON'T HAVE THE STRENGTH TO GO BACK.
LARRY. (*Stands.*)
AND HE LIFTED THE SHEEP ONTO HIS SHOULDERS
AND CARRIED IT BACK TO THE FLOCK. (*Sits.*)
PYRAMID PEOPLE. (CHILDREN *put bubu on* CRAIG.)
AND GOD SAID TO HIM:
SINCE YOU HAVE SUCH GREAT COMPASSION
TOWARD THIS FLOCK WHICH BELONGS TO
A MORTAL,
I SHALL ENTRUST TO YOU MY OWN FLOCK,
THE PEOPLE OF ISRAEL.
COMPANY. (CRAIG *crosses away from mountain towards center of space.*)
I DIDN'T KNOW YOU WERE THIRSTY.
YOU MUST BE VERY TIRED AFTER RUNNING SO FAR;

YOU DON'T HAVE THE STRENGTH TO GO BACK.
PETER. (*Stands.*)
IT TOOK GOD SEVEN DAYS TO CONVINCE HIM.
MOSES REFUSED.
CRAIG. (*In center with arms spread facing pyramid. Pyramid people reach out slowly to* CRAIG.)
WHY ME?
WHY NOT AN ANGEL?
OR MY OLDER BROTHER AARON?
I'M A POOR SPEAKER.
AND FURTHERMORE,
WHAT AM I SUPPOSED TO TELL THE JEWS
WHEN THEY START ASKING QUESTIONS,
SO MANY QUESTIONS? WHAT SHALL I SAY?
AND WHAT SHALL I TELL THE PHARAOH.
COMPANY. (ALL *drop arms.* MARTIN *leaves pyramid to get* MOSES *head.* RICHARD, ANTHONY *leave to get into Sorcerer's costumes. Rest of pyramid people cross slowly onto floor. They hold masks out in front.*)
YET IN THE END
HE GAVE IN.
GOD ALWAYS WINS.
PETER.
THE LAST WORD IS ALWAYS HIS
COMPANY.
AS WAS THE FIRST.
PETER. (*Stands and crosses to* CRAIG *and kneels.*)
ALSO CONSIDER THE SETTING:
PETER & STEVE. (STEVE *joins* PETER.)
THE FLAMING BUSH IN THE IMMENSITY OF
THE DESERT:
PETER, STEVE & RICHARD. (RICHARD *joins them.* CHILDREN *cross to places off mountain.*)
THE ALL-PERVASIVE SOLITUDE, THE ANXIETY,
PETER, STEVE, RICHARD, & LARRY. (*Pointing to Burning Bush which is located behind scrim at West end.*)
THE VOICE BOTH DISTANT AND CLOSE,
INSISTING, PROBING, THROBBING, BURNING.
HOW COULD ANY HUMAN BEING,
EVEN MOSES,
RESIST THAT VOICE INDEFINITELY.

BURNING BUSH

(*During the following,* MARTIN *enters from East End, goes to* CRAIG *and the two of them walk to mountain where* CRAIG *helps* MARTIN *put on "Moses" mask.* ALL *face Burning Bush.*)

COMPANY.
YAIEE YAIEE
YAIEE YAIEE
YAIEE YAIEE
YAIEE YAIEE
YAIEE YAIEE
YAIEE YAIEE

ADULTS.	CHILDREN.
YAIEE YAIEE YAIEE YAIEE	YAI YAI YAI YAI YAI
YAIEE YAIEE YAIEE YAIEE	YAI YAI YAI YAI YAI YAI
YAIEE YAIEE YAIEE YAIEE	YAI
YAIEE YAIEE YAIEE YAIEE	YAI YAI YAI YAI YAI
YAIEE YAIEE YAIEE YAIEE	YAI YAI YAI YAI YAI YAI
YAIEE . . .	YAI
YAIEE . . .	YAI YAI YAI YAI
YAIEE . . .	YAI YAI YAI YAI
YAIEE . . .	YAI YAI YAI YAI
YAIEE . . .	YAH AH
YAIEE . . .	AH AH
	AH AH
	AH

(MOSES *lifts his arms.*)

(*During the following,* MARTIN *lifts* CRAIG *onto hip, carries him around space, back to foot of mountain.*)

CHORUS. (*Rocking rhythmically.*)	CRAIG (*Shouted.*)
SHAL NA AH LE CHAH	ANAKNU MOSHRE
ME AL RA GLE CHAH	WE ARE MOSES
KI HA AH D'MAH	ANAKNU MOSHRE
AH SHER	WE ARE MOSES
AH TAH	ANAKNU MOSHRE
OH MED	WE ARE MOSES
BA BA BA BA	ANAKNU MOSHRE
	WE ARE MOSES

CHORUS.
A——
D'MAS
KO —
DESH
HI I I I I I I I I I
OOOO OOOO OOOO OOOO
OOOO

LARRY.
TZAY AKAT
YISRAEL BAA
ELA – EEE
TZAY AKAT
YISRAEL BAA
ELA – EEE

(MOSES *gestures to Burning Bush.*)

LARRY. (*Stands. Spoken under final oooo oooo.*)
LEAVING THE CALM OF THE DESERT,
MOSES PLUNGED INTO THE WHIRLPOOL OF
HISTORY.

(CRAIG *gives staff to* MOSES.)

NARRATION 3

(*During first 16 drum beats, large Pharaoh head is revealed on
    top of pyramid. During second 16 drum beats, entire
    COMPANY walks to East End of hall to confront Pharaoh.*)

JOSSIE. (*Jumps out of group and sings, then jumps back to
place.*)
THE MEETING BETWEEN MOSES
AND THE PHARAOH WAS STORMY.
ONNI. (*Jumps out of group and sings, then jumps back to
place.*)
MOSES AND HIS BROTHER AARON
CHALLENGED THE PHARAOH:
COMPANY. (*With arms in front of foreheads.*)
IN THE NAME OF THE GOD OF ISRAEL,
WE ASK YOU TO LET OUR PEOPLE GO.
B SHEM ELOKE YISRAEL
SHALACH ET AMIN

(*Shouted.* ALL *turn back and forth on one foot, looking from
    Pharaoh to* MOSES.)
B SHEM ELOKE YISRAEL
SHALACH ET AMIN

(ALL *sit. As each person sings or shouts the following he or she steps up on moat and faces group then jumps back down.*)

SHEILA. (*Sung.*)
THE PHARAOH ASKED ANGRILY:
LOUISE. (*Shouted.*)
WHO IS THIS GOD YOU ARE REFERRING TO?
DAVID. (*Shouted.*)
WHAT IS HIS NAME?
LARRY. (*Shouted.*)
WHAT DOES HIS POWER CONSIST OF?
PETER. (*Shouted.*)
HOW MANY WARS HAS HE WON?
IRA. (*Shouted.*)
HOW MANY WARS HAS HE WON?
STEVE. (*Shouted.*)
HOW MANY WARS HAS HE WON?

PHARAOH'S CHANT

(GROUP *faces West and kneels on four drum beats. During chant* CRAIG *fights two sorcerers,* ANTHONY *and* RICHARD, *who enter on moats with magic staffs.*)

COMPANY.
S—S—S—TOOM
AH CHAH
S—S—S—S—TOOM
AH S—S—S—AH
SAN CHAH
S—S—S—S—KEH
S—S—S—S—NEH
AH CHAH
OH K—NAH K—K—K
RRRRR AH
S—S—S—S—HAH
S—S—S—S—HAH
CHE CH'O CH'O HAH
CHE CH'O CH'O HAH
TS TS TS KI TCHEM
TS TS TS KI TCHEM
TS TS TS KI TCHEM

(*Sorcerers jump down from moats and approach* CRAIG *who fends them off with staff.*)

S−S−S−S−THYAT
S−S−S−S NEH VA
AH TA S−S−S−S−TOOM KS KS KS
AH TA S−S−S−S−TOOM KS KS KS
CHE KS KS KS AH VA ARA
CHE KS KS KS AH VA ARA
S−S−S−S NEH VA
S−S−S−S NEH VA
AH T D K GHA ZSH ZSH ZSH
AH T D K GHA ZSH ZSH ZSH
AH T D K GHA ZSH ZSH ZSH
AH T D K GHA ZSH ZSH ZSH
S−S−S−S NEH VA
S−S−S−S NEH VA
S−S−S−S TOOM
AH CHA
S−S−S−S TOOM
S−S−S−S TOOM
AH CHA
S−S−S−S TOOM.
S−S−S−S TOOM
AH CHA
S−S−S−S TOOM.

(*Sorcerers exit.*)

ZVEE. (*Enters from* S.E. *and reads to* CRAIG.) (*Flute Underscore.*)
Moses tried to explain the inexplicable −
That divine power has nothing
To do with human ambitions;
It fills the universe
And dominates the elements:
It is he who every day decides −
Me yechye oome yamut
Who shall live and who shall die.

(ZVEE *looks up at Pharaoh and then back at* CRAIG.)

But the Pharaoh was not persuaded.

(ZVEE *takes staff from* CRAIG.)

WHY HAST THOU DONE EVIL?

CHORUS. (*Stands up and walks slowly toward West End spreading out to cover whole floor as they walk.*)
OH LORD, WHY HAST THOU DONE EVIL TO THIS PEOPLE?

SHAMI & SHEILA.
WHY HAST THOU DONE EVIL TO THIS PEOPLE?

(CRAIG *turns and looks at* MOSES *who is kneeling.*)

CHORUS.
WHY DIDST THOU EVER SEND ME?
SHAMI & SHEILA.
WHY DIDST THOU EVER SEND ME?
CHORUS.
FOR SINCE I CAME TO PHARAOH
SHAMI & SHEILA.
FOR SINCE I CAME TO PHARAOH
CHORUS.
TO SPEAK IN THY NAME
SHAMI & SHEILA.
TO SPEAK IN THY NAME
CHORUS.
HE HAS DONE EVIL TO THIS PEOPLE
SHAMI & SHEILA.
HE HAS DONE EVIL TO THIS PEOPLE
CHORUS.
AND THOU HAST NOT DELIVERED THY PEOPLE AT ALL.

(MOSES *stands and exits* S.W.)

CRAIG.
And so God made Himself known to Pharaoh.
By punishing him.
MICHAEL.
With plagues.

(ALL *turn out.* ZVEE *enters* N.W.)

DOM — SPOKEN

ALL:	Dom
ZVEE:	Blood
ALL:	Tz'fardayah

ZVEE:	Frogs
ALL:	Keeneem
ZVEE:	Rats
ALL:	Orov
ZVEE:	Beasts
ALL:	Dever
ZVEE:	Disease
ALL:	Sh'cheen
ZVEE:	Boils
ALL:	Borod
ZVEE:	Hail
ALL:	Arbeh
ZVEE:	Locusts
ALL:	Choshech
ZVEE:	Darkness
ALL:	Makas b'choros
ZVEE:	Death of the first born.

LET MY PEOPLE GO

(*In between each speech, company makes quick dashes towards exits but are stopped as next speech begins (like the game* STATUES.). *Gradually different members of* COMPANY *make it to exits and disappear until at the last speech, only* SHAMI, ESTHER *and* SHEILA *remain.*)

ONNI. (ALL *say underlined words as they are spoken.*)
Let my people go
That they may serve me.
For this time I will
Send all my plagues
Upon your heart
And upon your servants
And your people
That you may know that there is
None like me
In all the earth.
DAVID. (ALL *say underlined words.*)
Take your rod
And stretch out your hand

Over the waters of Egypt
Over their rivers
Their canals and their ponds
And all their pools of water
That they may become blood.

LOUISE. (ALL *say underlined words.*)
Stretch out your hand
With your rod
Over the rivers
Over the canals
And over the pools
And cause frogs
To come upon the land of Egypt.

STEVE. (ALL *say underlined words.*)
Stretch out your rod
And strike the dust
Of the earth
That it may become gnats
Throughout all the land of Egypt.

IRA. (ALL *say underlined words.*)
Wait for the pharaoh
And say to him—
"If you will not
Let my people go
I will send
Swarms of flies on you."

ANTHONY. (ALL *say underlined words.*)
Behold the hand of the Lord
Will fall with a very severe plague
Upon your cattle
Which are in the field.

RICHARD. (ALL *say underlined words.*)
Take handfuls of ashes
From the kiln
Throughout all the land of Egypt
And boils

Shall break out on <u>man and beast</u>

   SHEILA. (ALL *say underlined words.*)
Stretch out your hand

Upon the land of <u>Egypt</u>

For the <u>locusts</u>

That they may come
Upon the land of <u>Egypt</u>

And eat every <u>plant in the land</u>.

   MICHAEL. (ALL *say underlined words.*)
Stretch out your <u>hand</u>

Towards <u>heaven</u>

That there be <u>darkness</u>

Over the land of <u>Egypt</u>

A <u>darkness to be felt</u>.

   SHAMI. (ALL *say underlined words.*)
I will go forth

In the midst of <u>Egypt</u>

And all the
<u>First born in the land of Egypt</u>

<u>Shall die</u>.

DOM — SUNG

(*Four drum beats to establish tempo — then:*)

   SHAMI & ESTHER.
DOM
  COMPANY.
DOM
   SHAMI & ESTHER.
TZ'FARDAYAH
  COMPANY.
TZ'FARDAYAH
   SHAMI & ESTHER.
KEENEEM
  COMPANY.
KEENEEM
   SHAMI & ESTHER.
OROV
  COMPANY.
OROV

SHAMI & ESTHER.
DEVER
  COMPANY.
DEVER
  SHAMI & ESTHER.
SH'CHEEN
  COMPANY.
SH'CHEEN
  SHAMI & ESTHER.
BOROD
  COMPANY.
BOROD
  SHAMI & ESTHER.
ARBEH
  COMPANY.
ARBEH
  SHAMI & ESTHER.
CHOSHECH
  COMPANY.
CHOSHECH
  SHAMI & ESTHER.
MAKAS B'CHOROS
COMPANY.
MAKAS B'CHOROS

PLAGUES

(*FROGS: Horny toad appears* D.R. *screen pulsating in and out of focus. Little frog appears* D.C. (R.) *swims up and down pattern: Big frog appears feet first* U.L. *(Horny toad and little frog continue activities). Big frog sticks out tongue. Big frog turns somersault—to position with feet* D.L. *Big frog leaps* U.R. *and returns to crouch with feet* D.L. *Big frog sticks out tongue (little frog end* U.L.*). Children cry.*)

CONCH—then: (*Four drums beats to establish tempo— then:*)

DOM—SUNG

  SHAMI & ESTHER.
DOM
  COMPANY.
DOM

SHAMI & ESTHER.
TZ'FARDAYAH
 COMPANY.
TZ'FARDAYAH
 SHAMI & ESTHER.
KEENEEM
 COMPANY.
KEENEEM
 SHAMI & ESTHER.
OROV
 COMPANY.
OROV
 SHAMI & ESTHER.
DEVER
 COMPANY.
DEVER
 SHAMI & ESTHER.
SH'CHEEN
 COMPANY.
SH'CHEEN
 SHAMI & ESTHER.
BOROD
 COMPANY.
BOROD
 SHAMI & ESTHER.
ARBEH
 COMPANY.
ARBEH
 SHAMI & ESTHER.
CHOSHECH
 COMPANY.
CHOSHECH
 SHAMI & ESTHER.
MAKAS B'CHOROS
COMPANY.
MAKAS B'CHOROS

(*During above DOM,* CRAIG *hands baskets, other items to* ESTHER, SHAMI *and* SALLY *at center of space.*)

(*DISEASE:* CAMEL *appears* R. — *begins to limp across screen when about midway* STEER *appears* U.L. *Almost immediately*

CAMEL *collapses—tries to get up, collapses again as* STEER *kicks back feet several times. Then* STEER *turns half somersault—rolls over and dies.)*

Interrupt with:

SHAMI. (*Chant.*)	ESTHER. (*Chant. Reads Hebrew passage from Haggadah.*)
CHAD GADYA, CHAD GADYA	
DIZBAN ABBA BITREI ZUZEI	
CHAD GADYA, CHAD GADYA	DOM VAYESH
	VETIMROT ASHAN
V'ATA SHUNRA V'OCHLA	DOM VAYESH
L'GADYA	VETIMROT ASHAN
DIZBAN ABBA BITREI ZUZEI	DOM (etc.)
CHAD GADYA, CHAD GADYA	

(*During above chant, three women walk west with baskets,* CRAIG *gets shawl and follows them.*)

(*BEASTS:* N.S.*—* VICTIM *appear* D.R. x L. *when at* C. LION *appear* R. LION *reach with claw and toss victim up.* VICTIM *somersaults.* LION *tosses him again and catches him in mouth. Out of Focus, then* VICTIM II *appear.* LION *reappear.* LION *toss* VICTIM. LION *catch* VICTIM *in paw.*

S.S.*—* VICTIM *appear* D.L. x R. BIRD *appear above, swooping.* VICTIM *begin* x L. BIRD *peck at* VICTIM. BIRD *pick up* VICTIM*—toss him so he falls turning somersault.* VICTIM II *appears.* BIRD *pick up with claws.*)

Interrupt with:

SHAMI. (*Chant.*)	ESTHER. (*Chant. During chant* CRAIG *puts shawl on women.*)
V'ATA CHALBA V'NASHACH	
L'SHUNRA	
D'OCHAL L'GADYA, DIZBAN	DOM VAYESH
ABBA BITREI ZUZEI	VETIMROT ASHAN
CHAD GADYA, CHAD GADYA	DOM VAYESH
	VETIMROT ASHAN
V'ATA CHUTRA V'HIKA	DOM (etc.)
L'CHALBA	
DNASHACH L'SHUNRA,	
D'OCHAL L'GADYA	
DIZBAN ABBA BITREI ZUZEI	
CHAD GADYA, CHAD GADYA	

(*LOCUSTS:* LOCUSTS *appear out of focus swarming in (Thunder sheet).* Locusts *splat on screen (drum sticks).* Locusts *swarm out of focus (thunder sheet).)*

CONCH — sounds, then: (*Four drums beats and:*)
DOM — SUNG

SHAMI & ESTHER.
DOM
  COMPANY.
DOM
  SHAMI & ESTHER.
TZ'FARDAYAH
  COMPANY.
TZ'FARDAYAH
  SHAMI & ESTHER.
KEENEEM
  COMPANY.
KEENEEM
  SHAMI & ESTHER.
OROV
  COMPANY.
OROV
  SHAMI & ESTHER.
DEVER
  COMPANY.
DEVER
  SHAMI & ESTHER.
SH'CHEEN
  COMPANY.
SH'CHEEN
  SHAMI & ESTHER.
BOROD
  COMPANY.
BOROD
  SHAMI & ESTHER.
ARBEH
  COMPANY.
ARBEH
  SHAMI & ESTHER.
CHOSHECH
  COMPANY.
CHOSHECH
  SHAMI & ESTHER.
MAKAS B'CHOROS

COMPANY.
MAKAS B'CHOROS

(*During above* DOM, *women walk east together.* CRAIG *waits at West side for rats and when they appear he walks with them as they move.*)

(*RATS:* RATS *appear far* R. *screen and cross* L. *across all screens taking little nibbles at other animals as they go. When* RATS *reach last screen — organ chord and voices pick up chord.*)
COMPANY.

AH . . .
SHAMI.
ADOSHEM ADOSHEM LAWMAW HAREOHSHAW
LAWOHM HAZEH, ADOSHEM ADOSHEM

(*Four drum beats and:*)

DOM — SUNG

SHAMI & ESTHER.
DOM
COMPANY.
DOM
SHAMI & ESTHER.
TZ'FARDAYAH
COMPANY.
TZ'FARDAYAH
SHAMI & ESTHER.
KEENEEM
COMPANY.
KEENEEM
SHAMI & ESTHER.
OROV
COMPANY.
OROV
SHAMI & ESTHER.
DEVER
COMPANY.
DEVER
SHAMI & ESTHER.
SH'CHEEN
COMPANY.
SH'CHEEN

SHAMI & ESTHER.
BOROD
  COMPANY.
BOROD
  SHAMI & ESTHER.
ARBEH
  COMPANY.
ARBEH
  SHAMI & ESTHER.
CHOSHECH
  COMPANY.
CHOSHECH
  SHAMI & ESTHER.
MAKAS B'CHOROS
  COMPANY.
MAKAS B'CHOROS

(*DARKNESS: As the musicians play all gongs, the* COMPANY
reenters and stands at both ends of the theatre in darkness.
CRAIG *stands in center and* ZVEE *and* SALLY *approach him*
for DEATH OF THE FIRST BORN. SALLY *places Egyptian*
hat on CRAIG.)

ALL. (*Whisper. Repeat every 4 beats during following spoken*
passage.)
Machas b choros
Machas b choros
  ZVEE.
Un Moishe hot gerufen aleh elster
Fun yisroeil un tzu zeh gezogt.
  SALLY.
Then Moses called all the elders of Israel and said to them.
  ZVEE.
tzit a roist, un nemteich schoff
loit ai reh mishpoches un shecht
dem korbn Pesach
  SALLY.
Select lambs for yourselves according to your families and kill
the passover lamb.
  ZVEE.
Un ir zolt nehmen a bintl eizev-gros
Un aintunken in dem blut voss in becken
Un ir zolt tzuriren tzu dem oiberstidl

Un tzu di beide bai stidlach fun dem
    blut vos in becken
    SALLY.
Take a bunch of hyssop and dip it in the blood which is in the
basin and touch the lintel and the two doorposts with the blood
which is in the basin.
    ZVEE.
Un ir zolt keine nisht a roiz gehen
fun dem aingang Fun zain hoiz bis inder
fri un az gott vet duch gehen tzu
    shlogn Mitzrayim
    SALLY.
And none of you shall go out of the door of his house until morn-
ing. For the Lord will pass through to slay the Egyptians.
    ZVEE.
Vet er zen dos blut oifn oiberstidl
Un oich di beide baishtidlech
    SALLY.
And when He sees the blood on the lintel and the two doorposts
    ZVEE.
Un gott vet iber hipn ibern eingang
Un a vett nit lossn dem umbrenger
Arain tzekumen in eihe hois tzu shlogn
    SALLY.
The Lord will pass over the door and will not allow the destroyer
to enter your houses to slay you.(SALLY *and* ZVEE *exit slowly.*)

(*ANGEL OF DEATH:* ANGEL *appears from East end of space,
    a large rod puppet manipulated by two men.* CRAIG *feels the
    presence of the* ANGEL *and turns to look at it. The* ANGEL
    *passes East to West slowly over him high up. He watches it
    and shields himself, raising his hands. The* ANGEL *turns at
    the East end and everyone starts sounds of the* ANGEL — *airy
    sounds of flapping, high siren-like sounds. The* ANGEL
    sweeps faster and lower over CRAIG *from East to West.*
    CRAIG *cries out and sinks to his knees. The* ANGEL *turns at
    the West and sweeps low over* CRAIG *who falls back, cries
    and dies. The* ANGEL *turns and comes back, very low, almost
    touching* CRAIG. *It hovers for a second. Then it lifts high and
    starts exit.*)

    JOSSIE. (*Then* ESTHER *and* OTHERS.)
YA NIBNE YA NIBNE

(MICHAEL *and* SHEILA, ANTHONY *and* LOUISE, DAVID *and* SALLY, STEVE *and* VICTOR *walk into center of space when "Ya Nibne" starts. One member of each couple picks up the other and spins him or her around during singing. Slow down and move back to groups as they hear violin note. During following, everyone is on floor with faces and hands down, facing center.*)

LOOK AT THE CHILDREN

SHAMI. (*Sings standing at East End. Violinist appears at West End. They face each other.*)
LOOK AT THE CHILDREN,
LOOK AT THEIR FACES,
LOOK AT THEM WELL,
THEY FILL THE WORLD.
INVADED THE HEAVENS.
INVADED, THE SOURCE.
INVADED, TOO,
YOUR EYES.
THESE CHILDREN,
HAVE TAKEN YOUR COUNTENANCE,
O GOD.
WHAT IS THE WORLD?
A GHETTO.
WHAT IS MAN?
A FUGITIVE,
A FUGITIVE LEAVING
ONE GHETTO FOR ANOTHER.
THE SOUL?
A FAINT SMILE
ON THE LIPS
OF A HUNGRY CHILD.
THE VOICE?
THAT SMILE'S SHADOW.
MEMORY?
THAT SHADOW'S SHADOW.
GOD?
YOU ARE IN THOSE EYES.
YOU BLIND THEM.
AND I LOOK
AT OUR CHILDREN BELOW
AND I SAY TO MYSELF:
THEY ARE ALONE,

TERRIBLY ALONE.
AND I LOOK
AT OUR CHILDREN BELOW
AND I SAY TO MYSELF:
THEY ARE SILENT,
TERRIBLY SILENT.

ZVEE. (*Enters* N.W. *to front of mountain.*)
Vayaas paro kidvar adoshem v'shalac et
B'nei yisrael meartzo.

PETER. (*Spoken.*)
When Pharaoh saw the death of his own son, he finally relented
and let the children of Israel go.

IRA. (*Standing on* S.E. *corner of pyramid.*)
RISE UP
GO FORTH FROM AMONG MY PEOPLE.
BOTH YOU AND THE PEOPLE OF ISRAEL.
AND GO SERVE THE LORD
AS YOU HAVE SAID.
TAKE YOUR FLOCKS AND YOUR HERDS
AS YOU HAVE ALSO SAID.
AND BEGONE
AND BLESS ME ALSO.
WE
ARE
ALL
DEAD
MEN.
WE ARE ALL DEAD MEN.

(IRA & TONY *lower the Pharaoh slowly until it is almost closed up
into the pyramid and then they slam it shut.* COMPANY *exits
quickly on 3 celeste glissandos.*)

PUPPET REBBE

MARTIN. (*Enters from behind pyramid, runs to center of
space.*)
Listen to a story! It is said of our ancient rabbis that they sat at a
table once, in b'nai b'rak and talked through the night about the
wonders of the liberation from Egypt. They talked so long and
so fervently that finally their students broke in on them and said:
"Gentlemen, gentlemen, it is time for morning prayer."

(*During percussion section, actors move out tables and chairs
and puppets and arrange then for PUPPET REBBE. The*

rebbe is done with puppets sitting around tables, men at large table, women at small table. Men have Haggadahs and women, cookbooks.)

EMMA. (ANTHONY.)
That's enough music. Take five. (SHE *hums "Take 5".*) Oh, little boy, come here, quick. Close your eyes. I have a surprise for you. Psst.

ALL.
One, two, three . . . Good Pesach.

CRAIG.
Sally, Sally (SALLY *enters.* CRAIG *runs around table greeting each male puppet. The female puppets sing.*)

POPE. (IRA.)
Gentlemen, let us turn to our Haggadahs.

EMMA. (ANTHONY.)
Ladies, let us turn to our cookbooks.

POPE. (IRA.)
Who would like to read?

MAX. (MARTIN.)
I will. He always reads. Rabbi Josef, the Galilean says, "How can you infer that the Egyptians were afflicted with ten plagues in Egypt, and on the sea with fifty plagues?"

ESTELLE. (LOUISE.)
Ten plagues? Who said ten plagues? I didn't see ten plagues, did you?

EMMA. (ANTHONY.)
No. What happened to the boils?

POPE. (IRA.)
How can you infer that the Egyptians were afflicted with ten plagues?

SARAH. (ONNI.)
Three medium cooking apples, one pound, preferably McIntosh or Northern spy.

ESTELLE. (LOUISE.)
One half cup chopped walnuts.

SARAH. (ONNI.)
One half teaspoon powdered ginger.

HYMIE. (DAVID.)
Turn to Exodus, Chapter 8-15. Quote . . .

ALL.
Epis

HYMIE. (DAVID.)

And the Magician said to Pharaoh, quote . . .

ALL.

Epis

HYMIE. (DAVID.)

This is the finger of God, unquote.

EBAN. (STEVE.)

And on the sea, what does it say?

HYMIE. (DAVID.)

Quote

ALL.

Epis

HYMIE. (DAVID.)

And Israel saw the great hand which the eternal laid upon the Egyptians.

EMMA. (ANTHONY.)

Peel, core, and chop the apples moderately coarse. Toss with walnuts . . .

ESTELLE. (LOUISE.)

No, you don't add the walnuts yet. I'm sure that comes later. (*To audience.*) Do you add the walnuts now or later?

MAX. (MARTIN.)

Now if by the finger they were afflicted with ten plagues, you can infer from this that in Egypt . . .

HYMIE. (DAVID.)

That's where the word finger is used.

EBAN. (STEVE.) They were smitten with ten plagues. And on the sea . . .

HYMIE. (DAVID.)

That's where the word hand is used.

SARAH. (OMNI.)

Pour in one half cup water and begin to stir in the flour gradually, using your fingertips or a fork . . . Stop looking at me!

ESTELLE. (LOUISE.)

Isn't she wonderful? She's my daughter.

EMMA. (ANTHONY.)

She's a g'dilla in the pupick. (*She sings a Yiddish song.*)

MAX. (MARTIN.)

They were smitten with fifty plagues.

EBAN. (STEVE.)

Rabbi Eliazar says, and I quote . . .

ALL.

Epis.

EBAN. (STEVE.)

How can we infer that each plague which the Holy One . . .
ALL.

Blessed be He.
EBAN. (STEVE.)

Brought upon the Egyptians was equivalent to four plagues?
POPE. (IRA.)

It is said . . .
HYMIE. (DAVID.)

In Psalm 78–49 . . .
POPE. (IRA.)

He sent forth upon them . . .
MEN.

The fierceness of his anger . . .
WOMEN.

Whoo
MEN.

Wrath . . .
WOMEN.

Ah
MEN.

Indignation . . .
WOMEN.

Oh
MEN.

Trouble . . .
WOMEN.

Oo
MEN.

And a sending of messengers of evil.

MEN.

Wrath . . .
EBAN. (STEVE.)

Denotes one plague.
MEN.

Indignation . . .
EBAN. (STEVE.)

Two.
MEN.

Trouble . . .
EBAN. (STEVE.)

Three.

EMMA. (ANTHONY.)

Ladies
WOMEN.

One quarter to one half teaspoon ground cinnamon. One and half tablespoons sugar or to taste. Three tablespoons red concord grape wine. I go with the wine.

MEN.
And a sending of messengers of evil . . .
  EBAN. (STEVE.)
Four.
  MAX. (MARTIN.)
Now young man, have you got that.
  CRAIG.
Yes.
  MAX. (MARTIN.)
Let's see. Wrath denotes how many plagues?
  CRAIG.
One plague.
  MAX. (MARTIN.)
Indignation?
  CRAIG.
Two.
  MAX. (MARTIN.)
A sending of messengers of evil?
  CRAIG.
Four.

(*Men show their approval.*)

  MAX. (MARTIN.)
Trouble?
  CRAIG.
Three.
  WILLY. (LARRY.)
Very good boy. That's a cute kid. I've seen cute . . . But he's
cute. Take this Yarmalke.
  EBAN. (STEVE.)
Hence it is to be inferred that in Egypt, they were smitten with
forty plagues.
  WILLY. (LARRY.)
And at the sea with two hundred plagues.
  ESTELLE. (LOUISE.)
That's a lot of plagues.
  EMMA. (ANTHONY.)
Did you see any boils? I didn't see boils. I saw frogs and rats
and . . . (puppets) . . .
  POPE. (IRA.)
Rabbi Akiba says, and I quote . . .

ALL.

Epis.

POPE. (IRA.)

How can we infer that each plague which the Holy One . . .

ALL.

Blessed be He.

POPE. (IRA.)

Brought upon the Egyptians in Egypt was equivalent to five plagues?

ESTELLE. (LOUISE.)

Five? What happened to forty? What happened to two hundred? You're back at five?

EMMA. (ANTHONY.)

Boils? What happened to the boils?

No one ever listens to me.

POPE. (IRA.)

It is said, and I quote

ALL.

Epis

POPE. (IRA.)

He sent forth upon them . . .

EBAN. (STEVE.)

Come on now.

EBAN. (STEVE.) & CRAIG.

The fierceness of his anger . . .

MAX. (MARTIN.) & CRAIG.

His wrath . . .

POPE. (IRA.) & CRAIG.

His indignation . . .

WILLY. (LARRY.) & CRAIG.

His trouble . . .

HYMIE. (DAVID.) & CRAIG.

And a sending of messengers of evil.

ESTELLE. (LOUISE.)

I haven't got the slightest idea of what they're talking about. Do you?

SARAH. (ONNI.)

Sh. Mama. The men are thinking.

ESTELLE. (LOUISE.)

Oh. Thinking.

POPE. (IRA.)

Hence it is to be inferred that in Egypt . . .

ESTELLE. (LOUISE.)
Where else, Philadelphia?
   SARAH. (ONNI.)
Sh. Mama.
   EMMA. (ANTHONY.)
Don't talk to me about Philadelphia. I could tell you two a few
things about Philadelphia.
   SARAH. (ONNI.)
What happened in Philadelphia?
   POPE. (IRA.)
Hence it is to be inferred that in Egypt they were smitten with
fifty plagues, and at the sea with two hundred and fifty plagues.
   ESTELLE. (LOUISE.)
Two hundred and fifty plagues?
   EBAN. (STEVE.)
Two hundred and fifty plagues.
   ALL.
Two hundred and fifty plagues.
   EMMA. (ANTHONY.)
I should think one would be enough.
   EBAN. (STEVE.)
And now, let's sing.
   EMMA. (ANTHONY.)
Music . . . Hey, young lady, that's your cue.

(JUDY *enters with accordian . . . they sing DAYENU . . . they
   are interrupted with 3 conch blasts.*)

   ALL.
What was that? Did you hear that noise? etc.
   EMMA. (ANTHONY.)
Enough with these plagues. Let's get on to the part where the
Hebrews depart and the Red Sea parts.
   ALL. (*Groan.*)

                       NARRATION 4

(COMPANY *removes chairs, tables and puppets and gathers at
   East end of space facing West.*)

   ALL.
THE LAST NIGHT

THE LAST CHANCE
A NUMBER OF NON-JEWISH SLAVES AND EGYPTIANS
DECIDED TO JOIN THE MOVEMENT:
NEVER AGAIN WOULD THEY HAVE
SUCH AN OPPORTUNITY TO LEAVE.

BOUVEN ELECH MAHER
BOUVEN ELECH MAHER
BOUVEN ELECH MAHER
BOUVEN ELECH MAHER

(COMPANY *does take and freeze on running positions.*)

LET'S GO
LET'S GO FAST
LET'S GO FASTER
LET'S GO FAST.

ONE COULD SEE PEOPLE RUNNING
RUNNING BREATHLESSLY,
WITHOUT A GLANCE BACKWARD,
THEY WERE RUNNING
TOWARD THE SEA
WITHOUT A GLANCE BACKWARD.
AND THERE THEY CAME TO AN ABRUPT HALT, (ALL
stand straight.)
THIS WAS THE END,
DEATH WAS THERE.
    JOSSIE.
WAITING.
    CRAIG.
DON'T BE AFRAID,
GO INTO THE WATER
INTO THE WATER!
ENTER THE SEA
NOT AS FRIGHTENED FUGITIVES
BUT AS FREE MEN.

DAYENU CHANT

ESTHER. (*Jumps out to front of* COMPANY. ALL *repeat* "DAYENU" *at end of each phrase spoken by* ESTHER.)

ESTHER.   ALL.

Kama maalot tovot lamakom aleinu.
Ilu hotsiyanu mimitsrayim v'lo asa
vahem sh'fatim.   Dayenu
Ilu asa vahem sh'fatim v'lo asa
veilo-hei-hem.   Dayenu
Ilu asa vei-lo-hei-hem v'lo harag
et b'chorei-hem.   Dayenu
Ilu harag et b'chorei-hem v'-lo
natan lanu et mamonam.   Dayenu
Ilu natan lanu et mamonam v'lo
kara lanu et hayam.   Dayenu
Ilu kara lanu et hayam v'lo
ha-aviranu v'tocho becharava.   Dayenu
Ilu haaviranu v'tocho becharava
v'lo shika tsareinu b'tocho.   Dayenu
Ilu shika tsareinu b'tocho v'lo sipeik
tsarekeinu bamidbar arba-im shana.   Dayenu
Ilu sipeik tsarkeinu bamidbar
arba-im shana v'lo he-echi-lanu et
haman.   Dayenu
Ilu he-echi-lanu et haman v'lo
natan lanu et hashabat.   Dayenu
Ilu natan lanu et hashabat v'lo
keirvanu lifnei har sinai.   Dayenu
Ilu keirvanu lifnei har sinai v'lo
natan lanu et hatorah.   Dayenu
Ilu natan lanu et hatorah v'lo
hichnisanu l'erets yisraeil.   Dayenu
Ilu hichni-sanu l'erets yisraeil v'lo
vana lanu beit hab'chirah.   Dayenu

ZVEE. (*Enters and goes to* CRAIG.)
Un Moishe hot gessogt tzum folk,
Ihr zolt nicht moire hobn shteht un
zett di Y'hoshvah fun gott vos er
vett aich haint ton
And Moses turned to God with a prayer. But God reminded him
that this was *NOT* the right moment. (*With* CRAIG.) Tell the
people of Israel to hurry. (ZVEE *exits* N.W.)

PREPARATION FOR THE RED SEA

(COMPANY *joins hands and walks single file, while singing, in rhythm all the way around the hall. The ends of a large piece of rolled-up white silk, preset at West End of hall, are picked up by several actors and pulled to the East End to extend the silk the length of the floor. Long poles are attached to the silk at the four corners and at either side in the center.)*

COMPANY.
DA AH AH AH AH AH AH AH
YE EH EH EH EH EH EH EH
NU U U U U U U U
DA YE EH EH EH NU

	BOYS.	
DA AH AH AH AH AH AH AH	DA	
YE EH EH EH EH EH EH EH	YE	
NU U U U U U U U	NU	
DA YE EH EH EH NU	DAYENU	LARRY &
		JOSSIE.
DA AH AH AH AH AH AH AH	DA	DAYENU
YE EH EH EH EH EH EH EH	YE	DAYENU
NU U U U U U U	NU	DAYENU
DA YE EH EH EH NU	DAYENU	DAYENU
DA AH AH AH AH AH AH AH	DA	DAYENU
YE EH EH EH EH EH EH EH	YE	DAYENU
NU U U U U U U	NU	DAYENU
DA YE EH EH EH NU	DAYENU	DAYENU

(CRAIG *walks out on the silk from the East End. Pole handlers at West End flip the silk to create waves and* CRAIG *jumps over 4 or 5 waves. Then he motions to company to follow.)*

CROSSING THE RED SEA

(*Zither begins. As* COMPANY *crosses, sides of silk are raised so that audience sees silhouettes through silk.*)

COMPANY.
AH AH AH AH
AH AH AH AH

AH AH AH AH
AH AH AH AH

(*Add drone and harmony.*)

AH AH AH AH
AH AH AH AH
AH AH AH AH
AH AH AH AH

(*Add high harmony.*)

AH AH AH AH
AH AH AH AH
AH AH AH AH
AH AH AH AH

(*PERCUSSION: Pharaoh Crossing the Red Sea. As last member leaves silk, pole handlers raise silk into air and twist and toss material. Pharaoh and his men figure 8 around the space shaking their shields toward the audience. Then they form a line in the center and turn shields in a domino effect, L.R., L.R. Then they split, every person going to the same side and shaking shields toward audience four times. Then armies shake their shields L.R., L.R. repeating while RICHARD spins with Pharaoh head at West end. When RICHARD bellows and lifts Pharaoh high, everyone exits back to East end and the sea billows in behind them. SHEILA standing on the mountain grins in triumph at Pharaoh's defeat.*)

WHO IS LIKE UNTO THEE

SHEILA. (*Standing on mountain.*)
WHO IS LIKE UNTO THEE, OH LORD
    CHORUS. (*Appearing at East end with backs to mountain and slowly walking backwards towards mountain.*)
OH, LORD.
    SHEILA.
AMONG THE MIGHTY?
    CHORUS.
MIGHTY.

SHEILA.
WHO IS LIKE UNTO THEE, OH LORD.
  CHORUS.
LIKE THEE, OH LORD.
  SHEILA.
GLORIOUS IN HOLINESS?
  CHORUS.
GLORIOUS HOLINESS.
  SHEILA.
FEARFUL IN PRAISES
  CHORUS.
AH PRAISES.
  SHEILA.
DOING WONDERS.
  CHORUS.
AH WONDERS.
  SHEILA.
WHO IS LIKE UNTO THEE, OH LORD.
  CHORUS.
WHO IS LIKE THEE, OH LORD (*Turn and face mountain.*)
  SHEILA.
WHO IS LIKE UNTO THEE, OH LORD.
  CHORUS.
WHO IS LIKE THEE, OH LORD.

  ALL. (*Approach mountain in single file and climb upon it.*)
HOLY, HOLY, HOLY
THE WHOLE EARTH IS FULL OF HIS GLORY.

HOLY, HOLY, HOLY
THE WHOLE EARTH IS FULL OF HIS GLORY.

HOLY, HOLY, HOLY
THE WHOLE EARTH IS FULL OF HIS GLORY.

HOLY, HOLY, HOLY
THE WHOLE EARTH IS FULL OF HIS GLORY.

(*Begin clapping.*)

HOLY, HOLY, HOLY
THE WHOLE EARTH IS FULL OF HIS GLORY.

HOLY, HOLY, HOLY
THE WHOLE EARTH IS FULL OF HIS GLORY.

HOLY, HOLY, HOLY
THE WHOLE EARTH IS FULL OF HIS GLORY.

HOLY, HOLY, HOLY
THE WHOLE EARTH IS FULL OF HIS GLORY.

(*Stop clapping.*)

AH AH AH AH AH AH MEN.
    SHAMI. (*Shouted—Standing on pyramid at East end.* COM-
PANY *turns away covering face.*)
Maase yadai tovim bayam veatem
Omrim shira?
    LARRY. (*Slowly, one by one,* COMPANY *looks at* SHAMI.)
Was this the moment of grace? The whole world became song.
Even the angels began to sing, but God interrupted them with
the most universally human call to order in the Talmud.
    SHAMI.
Maase yadai tovim bayam veatem omrin shira?
My creatures are drowning in the sea . . .
And you are singing?
What if they are enemies of Israel and liberty . . .
They are still human beings.
How can you think of singing while human beings
Are drowning? (ALL *sit on piano vamp.*)

NARRATION 5

    SHAMI. (*Sits on pyramid.*)
THEN, SEVEN WEEKS LATER,
CAME THE BIG MOMENT,
THE UNIQUE EVENT
IN THE MEMORY OF MANKIND:
GOD WAS ABOUT TO SPEAK,
TO REVEAL HIS LAW
TO MAKE HIS VOICE HEARD.
THEN, ABRUBTLY,
THERE WAS SILENCE. (*4 beats of silence.*)

VICTOR & KERRY. (*Stand.*)
AND IN THIS SILENCE
A VOICE WAS HEARD.
GOD SPOKE. (*Sit.*)
    ALL.
WHAT DID HE SPEAK OF?
    IRA. (*Stand.*)
HIS SECRET WORK,
HIS ETERNALLY IMPERCEPTIBLE INTENTIONS? (*Sit.*)
    ALL.
NO.
    RICHARD. (*Stand.*)
HE SPOKE OF MAN'S RELATIONSHIP TO MAN, (*Sit.*)
    MICHAEL. (*Stand.*)
OF ONE INDIVIDUAL'S DUTIES TOWARD OTHERS.
(*Sit.*)
    LOUISE & ONNI. (*Stand.*)
AT THIS UNIQUE MOMENT
GOD WISHED TO DEAL
WITH HUMAN RELATIONS
RATHER THAN THEOLOGY. (LOUISE *sit.*)
    ONNI. (*Jumps off mountain and runs to center of space.*)
Listen to a midrash: (*Drum Beat.*) Among the children of Israel,
there were those who followed Moses with their eyes, saying:
Look at this neck and look at that belly and those legs: Whatever
he eats, he has taken from the Jews: Whatever he drinks, he has
taken from the Jews: Everything he owns comes from the Jews.
    STEVEN. (*Jumps off mountain and runs to center of space.*)
Listen to a midrash: (*Drum Beat.*) No sooner had they left Egypt
than they already asked to return: Why did you make us leave,
they asked Moses. Aren't there enough graves in Egypt? Why
do you want to bury us all in the desert?
    DAVID. (*Jumps off mountain and runs to center of space.*)
Listen to a midrash: (*Drum Beat.*) Three days after the miracu-
lous Red Sea crossing, all they wanted to know was: Ma niste?
What is there to drink? Barely one month later they recalled
Egypt with nostalgia: It was so good there: We ate all we
wanted . . .

SONG OF WAITING

(*As song is sung, everyone except* CRAIG *and* MARTIN (MOSES)
follows LARRY *and slowly descends from mountain and*

wanders around hall. By song's end, wanderers should be located in small group near center of hall facing outward.)

LARRY.
DON'T YOU WANT TO JUST LAY DOWN
FOUR MEMBERS OF COMPANY.
LAY DOWN
LARRY.
YOUR WEARY FEET.
COMPANY (4).
YOUR WEARY FEET.
LARRY.
AND REST YOUR WANDERINGS A WHILE
COMPANY (4).
AND REST YOUR WANDERINGS A WHILE
LARRY.
AND FIND THE FRUIT OF THE LAND
COMPANY (4).
AND FIND THE FRUIT OF THE LAND
LARRY.
DIDN'T THEY PROMISE US MANNA
COMPANY (4).
MANNA
LARRY.
FROM HEAVEN
COMPANY (4).
FROM HEAVEN
LARRY.
WATER FROM ROCKS AND RICH EARTH FROM THE SAND.
COMPANY (4).
WATER FROM ROCKS AND RICH EARTH FROM THE SAND.
LARRY.
I AM SO WEARY
COMPANY (4).
WEARY
LARRY.
FROM WANDERING
COMPANY (4).
FROM WANDERING
LARRY.
AND ALL THE PROMISES GONE.

COMPANY (4).
AND ALL THE PROMISES GONE.
LARRY.
I WANT TO GIVE UP
COMPANY (4).
GIVE UP
LARRY.
THIS JOURNEY
COMPANY (4).
THIS JOURNEY
LARRY.
AND FORGET WHAT WAS WON
COMPANY (4).
AND FORGET, AND FORGET WHAT WAS WON.

MICHAEL.	ALL.
AND THE LIGHT HAS TURNED TO DARK	HMMMM.
STEVEN.	
AND THE DREAMS HAVE TURNED TO	ALL.
HATE	HMMMM.
JOSSIE.	ALL.
AND THE LONELINESS WON'T GO AWAY.	HMMM

LARRY.
AND I'M WEARY
ALL.
WEARY
LARRY.
MISTRUSTFUL
ALL. (*In small group.*)
MISTRUSTFUL. AND I CAN'T FIND MY WAY. OH LORD
SHEILA.
HOW MANY CHILDREN MUST DIE
ALL.
OH LORD.
SHEILA.
HOW MANY NIGHTS OF WAITING
ALL.
OH LORD.
SHEILA.
HOW MANY DREAMS UNFULFILLED
ALL.
OH LORD
SHEILA.
HOW LONG WILL YOU

ALL.
TEST ME

ANTHONY. (*Breaks away from group.*)
Listen to a midrash. (*Drum Beat.*) At one point, Moses became
so exasperated that he cried out: (ALL *turn away, cover faces.*)
ANTHONY & CRAIG.
Oh God, what am I to do with this ungrateful people? One more
incident and they will stone me to death.
MICHAEL. (*On mountain.* COMPANY *spreads out at West end
of space.*)
STANDING AT THE TOP OF THE MOUNTAIN
THE TABLETS OF THE LAW IN HIS ARMS,
MOSES PERCEIVED AN UNWANTED NOISE
FROM DOWN BELOW.
HIS PEOPLE WERE DANCING,
REJOICING,
WORSHIPPING THE GOLDEN
CA------ALF.
ALL.
YI!

(MICHAEL *lifts* CRAIG *over head and walks down mountain and
through* COMPANY *to center of space.* COMPANY *falls on
knees on 8th beat of CALF.*)

THE GOLDEN CALF

COMPANY. (*On knees, do stylized dance.* RICHARD, DAVID *and*
LOUISE *do dance in front of* COMPANY *with* MICHAEL *holding*
CRAIG.)
YA BA BA BA BIM BAM BIM BAM BIM BAM
YA BA BA BA BIM BAM BIM BAM BIM
YA BA BA BA BIM BAM BIM BAM BIM BAM
YA BA BA BA BIM BAM BIM BAM BIM

YA BA BA BA BIM BAM BIM BAM BIM BAM
YA BA BA BA BIM BAM BIM BAM BIM

YA BA BA BA BIM BAM BIM BAM BIM BAM
YA BA BA BA BIM BAM BIM BAM BIM

LAI LAI LAI
LAI
LAI LAI LAI LAI
LAI LAI LAI LAI LAI

LAI LAI LAI
LAI
LAI LAI LAI LAI
LAI LAI LAI LAI LAI

LAI LAI LAI
LAI
LAI LAI LAI LAI
LAI LAI LAI LAI LAI

LAI LAI LAI
LAI
LAI LAI LAI LAI
LAI LAI LAI LAI LAI

(ALL *spin around space in ecstasy.*)

YA BUM BA BIM BA BA BUM
YA BUM BA BIM BA BA BUM

YA BUM BA BIM BA BA BUM
YA BUM BA BIM BA BA BUM

(COMPANY *falls to floor.*)

 MICHAEL. (*Cuts them off.*)
RRRAUGHRR
HIS DISAPPOINTMENT WAS BOUNDLESS
HE NEVER KNEW WHAT TO EXPECT
FROM HIS PEOPLE. (*Sets* CRAIG *down.*)

GOD OF MERCY

 PETER. (*Stands.*)
GOD OF MERCY
CHOOSE ANOTHER PEOPLE FOR A WHILE
 KERRY. (*Stands.*)
WE ARE TIRED OF DEATH AND DYING

WE HAVE NO MORE PRAYERS
CHOOSE ANOTHER PEOPLE FOR A WHILE
PETER.
WE HAVE NO MORE BLOOD LEFT TO BE VICTIMS
JOSSIE. (*On one knee.*)
OUR HOUSE IS TURNED INTO DESERT
THE EARTH LACKS SPACE FOR OUR GRAVES
COMPANY.
THERE ARE NO MORE LAMENTATIONS
OR SONGS OF WOE LEFT IN THE ANCIENT BOOKS
GOD OF MERCY
SANCTIFY ANOTHER LAND ANOTHER SINAI
WE HAVE COVERED EVERY FIELD AND STONE
WITH ASHES AND HOLINESS
WITH OUR OLD, WITH OUR YOUNG, AND WITH
OUR NEWLY BORN HAVE WE PAID
FOR EVERY LETTER IN YOUR TEN COMMANDMENTS

(ALL *sit facing mountain.*)

THE TEN COMMANDMENTS

ZVEE. (*Reads from book on mountain.* COMPANY *does stylized hand movements in rhythm depicting each of the 10 Commandments.*)

Anochi Adonai elohecha asher hotseiticha meierets mitsrayim mibeit avadim. Lo yi-yeh l'cha elohim acheirim al panai. Lo ta aseh l'cha fesel v'chol t'muna asher bashamayim mima-al va-asher ba-arets mitachat va-asher bamayim mitachat la-arets. Lo tishtachaveh lahem v'lo ta-avdeim ki anochi Adonai elohecha eil kana pokeid avon avot al banim al sh'leishim v'al ri-bei-im l'sonai.

V'oseh chesed la-alafim l'ohavai ul'shomrei mitsvotai.

Lo tisah et sheim Adonai elohecha la-shav ki lo y'nakeh Adonai eit yisah et sh'mo lashav. Zachor et yom hashabat l'kadsho. Shei-shet yamim tavod v'asitah kol m'lachtechah. V'yom ha-shvi-i shabat la'Adonai elohecha lo ta-aseh chol m'lacha atah uvincha uvitecha avd'cha va-a-mat'-cha uv'hemtecha v'geircha asher bishorecha. Ki sheishet yamim asa Adonai et hashamayim v'et ha-arets et hayam v'et kol asher bam vayanach ba yom hashvi-i al kein beirach Adonai et yom hashabat Vay'kadshei hu. Kabeid et avicha v'et imecha l'ma-an ya-arichun yamecha al ha-adam asher Adonai elohecha notein lach. Lo tirtsach. Lo tinaf. Lo tignov. Lo ta-aneh vreiacha eid shaker. Lo tachmod beit rei-echa. Lo tachmod eishet reiecha v'avdo va-amato v'shoro vachamoro v'chol asher l'reiecha.

AMEN

(MOSES *walks East through center of* COMPANY. ALL *rise as he passes them.*)
    ALL.
AH AH AH AH AH AH AH AH
AH AH AH AH AH AH AH AH
ME EH EH EH EH EH EH EN
AH AH AH AH MEN

AH AH AH AH AH AH AH AH
AH AH AH AH AH AH AH AH
ME EH EH EH EH EH EH EN
AH AH AH AH MEN

NARRATION 6
(COMPANY *exits and then enters with tables and chairs, places them in center of hall, then goes to positions on either side of hall, sit.*)

    ONNI.
IN SPITE OF HIS DISAPPOINTMENTS
IN SPITE OF HIS ORDEALS
AND THE LACK OF GRATITUDE HE ENCOUNTERED,
    ALL.
MOSES
NEVER
LOST HIS FAITH IN HIS PEOPLE.

SOMEHOW
HE FOUND
BOTH THE STRENGTH
AND THE COURAGE TO REMAIN ON ISRAEL'S SIDE
AND PROCLAIM ITS HONOR AND ITS RIGHT TO LIVE.

VAYIGDAL MOSHE VAYETZE EL ECHAV
VAYIGDAL MOSHE VAYETZE EL ECHAV
VAYIGDAL MOSHE VAYETZE EL ECHAV
VAYIGDAL MOSHE VAYETZE EL ECHAV

VICTOR, KERRY & SALLY. (*Standing on tables.* MOSES *on mountain blesses* ANTHONY, SHEILA, ESTHER, RICHARD, DAVID *and* LOUISE *in masks. At end of benediction, they exit.*)
MOSES SPENT HIS LAST HOUR
BLESSING ISRAEL'S TRIBES.
HE BEGAN BLESSING THEM ONE BY ONE
BUT TIME WAS RUNNING OUT
AND SO HE INCLUDED THEM
    ALL.
ALL IN ONE BENEDICTION.
    SHAMI & ZVEE.
Echod elohanu she ba sho mayim
U ho 'oritz
    ALL.
Our God is one in heaven and earth

KODOSH	CRAIG.
KODOSH	When Moses learned that his last
KODOSH	hour had come he refused to accept
KODOSH	it. He wanted to go on living. He put
KODOSH	on sackcloth, covered himself with
KODOSH	ashes and composed fifteen hundred
KODOSH	prayers. Then he drew a circle around
IRA.	himself and declared: I shall not
O NAW ADOSHEM	move from here. But God said — you
HO SHEE YAW NAW	must die, Moses, otherwise the people
ALL.	will turn you into an idol.
HO SHEE YAW	
NAW	

(MOSES *takes off mask and exits from mountain.*)

    IRA.
O NAW ADOSHEM HO SHEE YAW NAW
    ALL.
HO SHEE YAW NAW
    IRA.
O NAW ADOSHEM HATZLI CHAW NAW
    ALL.
HATZLI CHAW NAW
    IRA.
O NAW ADOSHEM HATZLI CHAW NAW
    ALL.
HATZLI CHAW NAW

KODOSH
KODOSH
KODOSH
KODOSH
KODOSH
KODOSH
KODOSH

(ALL *exit except* CRAIG *on mountain.*)

THE DEATH OF MOSES

CRAIG. (*On mountain.*)
NOBODY KNOWS HIS RESTING PLACE.
THE PEOPLE OF THE MOUNTAINS
SITUATE IT IN THE VALLEY.
THE PEOPLE OF THE VALLEY
SITUATE IT IN THE MOUNTAINS.
IT HAS BECOME NEITHER TEMPLE OR MUSEUM.
IT IS EVERYWHERE AND ELSEWHERE
ALL. (*From off-stage.*)
ALWAYS ELSEWHERE
ALWAYS ELSEWHERE
ALWAYS ELSEWHERE
SHAMI. (*Enters at East end, walks around table to* CRAIG *at West end who comes down off mountain to meet her.*)
NOBODY WAS PRESENT AT HIS DEATH.
AND SO, IN A WAY,
HE LIVES ON INSIDE US,
EVERY ONE OF US.
FOR AS LONG AS ONE CHILD OF ISRAEL,
SOMEWHERE,
PROCLAIMS HIS LAW AND HIS TRUTH,
MOSES LIVES ON THROUGH HIM,
IN HIM,
AS DOES THE BURNING BUSH,
WHICH CONSUMES MAN'S HEART
WITHOUT CONSUMING HIS FAITH.
CRAIG.
LAI LAI
SHAMI.
WHICH CONSUMES MAN'S HEART
WITHOUT CONSUMING HIS FAITH

CRAIG.
LAI LAI
SHAMI.
WHICH CONSUMES MAN'S HEART
WITHOUT CONSUMING HIS FAITH

A BLESSING

(*The following blessing is done very intimately,* SHAMI *stands
with* CRAIG *at* w. *end looking at table, then they cross to the
*e. *end and finish looking at table from that end. She kisses*
CRAIG *on the cheek at the end of the blessing and they exit*
N.E.)

SHAMI. (*Spoken.*)
Rebonoh shel olom, ich dank un loib deine leebn nomen vos du
hust mir g'geben lebn un koyach areintsubrengen dem leebn
yom-tov-pesach in shtub areine. Bahlt, vet men shoen bodek-
chometz-zeine, oys rahmen yeddher krishke foon deh binkelech
un shparunkelech. Zool es zeine deine viln, az meine mahn un
deh kinderlach, zolen lebn, deh gantza mishpawchaw, zolen
hubn deh scheeaw tsoo prahven deine ti-ye-ren yom tov in
nachas un in brocho alevai omein.

BEH DEE KAS CHOMETZ

WOMEN. (*Enter* N.E. *with service for table and set table during
song.*)
BEH DEE KAS CHOMETZ YA BA BOYM
BEH DEE KAS CHOMETZ YA BA BOYM
BEH DEE KAS CHOMETZ YA BA BOYM
BEH DEE KAS CHOMETZ
SHAMI.
LAI LAI LAI
LAI LAI LAI   2x

WOMEN.	BOYS.
BEH DEE KAS CHOMETZ YA BA BOYM	BEH DEE KAS CHOMETZ
BEH DEE KAS CHOMETZ YA BA BOYM	BEH DEE KAS CHOMETZ
BEH DEE KAS CHOMETZ YA BA BOYM	BEH DEE KAS CHOMETZ
BEH DEE KAS CHOMETZ	BEH DEE KAS CHOMETZ

ESTHER.
LAI LAI LAI
LAI LAI LAI ⟩ 2x

WOMEN.   BOYS.
BEH DEE KAS CHOMETZ   BEH DEE KAS CHOMETZ
YA BA BOYM
BEH DEE KAS CHOMETZ   BEH DEE KAS CHOMETZ
YA BA BOYM
BEH DEE KAS CHOMETZ   BEH DEE KAS CHOMETZ
YA BA BOYM
BEH DEE KAS CHOMETZ   BEH DEE KAS CHOMETZ

JOSSIE.
LAI LAI LAI
LAI LAI LAI ⟩ 2x

WOMEN.   BOYS.
BEH DEE KAS CHOMETZ   BEH DEE KAS CHOMETZ
YA BA BOYM
BEH DEE KAS CHOMETZ   BEH DEE KAS CHOMETZ
YA BA BOYM
BEH DEE KAS CHOMETZ   BEH DEE KAS CHOMETZ
YA BA BOYM
BEH DEE KAS CHOMETZ   BEH DEE KAS CHOMETZ

SHEILA, LOUISE, & ONNI.
LAI LAI LAI LAI
LAI LAI LAI LAI ⟩ 2x

WOMEN & BOYS. (*Finish   MEN. (*Enter in single file
setting table and form line at   carrying flowers and go to their
West end facing East.*)   places at table.*)
BEH DEE KAS CHOMETZ   YA BA BA BA BUM
YA BA BOYM   BUM BUM BUM BUM
BEH DEE KAS CHOMETZ   YA BA BA BA BUM
YA BA BOYM   BUM BUM BUM BUM
BEH DEE KAS CHOMETZ   YA BA BA BA BUM
YA BE BOYM   BUM BUM BUM BUM
BEH DEE KAS CHOMETZ   YA BA BA BA BUM
                                          BUM BUM BUM BUM
                                          YA BA BA BA BUM
                                          etc.

WOMEN. (*Join men.*)
LAI LAI LAI LAI
LAI LAI LAI LAI
LAI LAI LAI LAI
LAI LAI LAI LAI

ALL. (*Turn out to audience.* ZVEE *enters.*)
KOL DICH VEH N'YE TSE VEE ECHOL
KOL DITZ RE YAK N'YE TSE VEE ETZACH
KOL DICH VEH N'YE TSE VEE ECHOL
KOL DITZ RE YAK N'YE TSE VEE ETZACH
    ZVEE. (*At head of table.*)
Let anyone who is hungry come and eat.
Let anyone who is needy come and
Make passover with us. (COMPANY *sits.*)
    CRAIG. (*Stands on chair.*)
MA NISH TA NAH HA LAI LAH HAZEH
MIKOL HA LAY LOS?

ELIJAH

    ZVEE. & SHAMI. (ZVEE *reads and* SHAMI *sings softly in monotone repeating the lines* ZVEE *has just read—lines overlap.* ESTHER *stands behind* ZVEE *with cup raised and turns in circle.* CRAIG *leaves table in middle of recitation and walks slowly to top of mountain, timing his arrival to match end of speech.*)
A camp
An inmate.
A creature without a name,
A man without a face,
Without a destiny.
It is night,
The first night of passover.
The camp is asleep,
He alone is awake.
He talks to himself
Soundlessly.
I hear his words,
I capture his silence.
To himself, to me,
He is saying:
I have not partaken of matzoth,
Nor of moror.
I have not emptied the four cups,
Symbols of the four deliverances.
I did not invite
The hungry

Or even my hunger.

No longer have I a son
To ask me the four questions —
No longer have I the strength
To answer.
I say the Haggadah
And I know it lies.
The parable of Had-Gadya is false:
God will not come
To slay the slaughterer.
The innocent victims
Will go unavenged.
The ancient wish —
Leshana habaa bi — yerushalaim —
Will not be granted.
I shall not be in Jerusalem
Next year.
Or anywhere else.
Next year
I shall not be.

And then,
How do I know
That Jerusalem is there,
Faraway,
That Jerusalem is not here?
Still, I recite the Haggadah
As though I believe in it.
And I await the prophet Elijah,
As I did long ago.
I open my heart to him
and say:
Welcome, prophet of the promise,
Welcome, herald of redemption.
Come, share in my story,
Come, rejoice with the dead
That we are.
Empty the cup
That bears your name.
Come to us,
Come to us on this passover night:
We are in Egypt

And we are the ones
To suffer God's plagues.
Come, friend of the poor,
Defender of the oppressed,
Come.
I shall wait for you.
And even if you disappoint me
I shall go on waiting,
Ani maamin.

ESTHER. (*Sings to* CRAIG.)
ELIYAHU HANAVI
ELIYAHU HATISHBI
ELIYAHU HANAVI
ELIYAHU HAGILADI
BIMHERA V'YAMENU
YAVO ELEYNU
IM MASHIACH IM MASHIACH
IM MASHIACH BEN DAVID

(CRAIG *reaches top of mountain and opens door. Then turns to face hall and smiles.*)

SONG OF SONGS

CHILDREN. (*Standing on chairs.* CRAIG *comes down mountain and runs to his place at table.*)
ARISE, MY BELOVED
MY FAIR ONE
AND COME AWAY.
FOR LO,
THE WINTER IS PAST,
THE RAIN IS OVER AND GONE.
THE FLOWERS APPEAR ON THE EARTH
THE TIME OF SINGING OF BIRDS IS COME
AND THE VOICE OF THE TURTLE
IS HEARD IN OUR LAND.
THE FIG TREE PUTTETH FORTH HER GREEN FIGS
CHORUS.
LI LI LI LI
CHILDREN.
AND THE VINES WITH THE TENDER GRAPE
GIVE A GOOD SMELL

CHORUS.
LI LI LI
LI LI LI
LI LI LI
LI LI LI
CHILDREN.
ARISE MY LOVE MY FAIR ONE
CHORUS.
LI LI LI LI LI
CHILDREN.
AND COME AWAY
CHORUS.
LI LI LI LI LI

CHILDREN.	CHORUS.
OH MY DOVE THAT ART	LI LI, LI LI, LI LI,
IN THE CLEFTS OF THE ROCK	LI, LI LI
IN THE SECRET PLACES	LI LI LI LI, LI LI LI LI,
OF THE STAIRS	LI LI LI LI LI
LET ME SEE THY	LI LI, LI LI, LI LI,
COUNTENANCE,	LI, LI LI
LET ME HEAR THY VOICE	LI LI LI LI, LI LI LI LI,
FOR SWEET IS THY VOICE.	LI LI LI LI LI
	LI LI, LI LI, LI LI,
	LI, LI LI,
	LI LI LI LI, LI LI LI LI,
	LI LI LI LI LI LI

CHILDREN.
OH, THY COUNTENANCE IS COMELY.
CHORUS.
LI LI LI
LI LI LI
LI LI LI
LI LI LI
CHILDREN.
TAKE US THE FOXES
CHORUS.
LI LI LI LI LI
CHILDREN.
THE LITTLE FOXES,
CHORUS.
LI LI LI LI LI
CHILDREN.
THAT SPOIL THE VINES

CHORUS.
LI LI LI LI LI
    CHILDREN.   CHORUS.
MY BELOVED IS MINE   LI LI LI LI
AND I AM HIS.   LI LI LI LI
MY BELOVED IS MINE   LI LI LI LI
AND I AM HIS.   LI LI LI LI
   ZVEE.
La shana ha ba a bi y'rushalyaim
   ESTHER.
Amen.

CHORALE

(COMPANY *holding hands at table.*)

ARISE MY BELOVED MY FAIR ONE
AND COME AWAY.
FOR, LO, THE WINTER IS PAST,
THE RAIN IS OVER AND GONE.
AH . . .

(*Lights fade.*)

BOWS

THE END

The stage is a long rectangular room with pyramid and moats at East End and mountain at West End. Performers enter and exit from both sides on either end. Thus, there is a Northeast and Southeast EXIT/ENTRANCE and a Northwest and Southwest ENTRANCE/EXIT.

The plagues are depicted by special shadow puppets thrown on screens extending over the audience's heads. During the Puppet Rebbe, large life-size puppets are utilized. They are seated at the tables and are manipulated by the actors who sit below them on collapsible chairs.

The Angel of Death is a large rod puppet suspended from two long poles which are held up by two men.

The Moses mask is a large stylized head which fits over the actor's head and rests on his shoulders. Masks worn by the Pyramid People are plain facial masks which the actors hold up before their faces.

Pharaoh is depicted by a huge stylized head which is located on top of the pyramid and can be raised or lowered. His army is depicted by 6 hand carried shields.

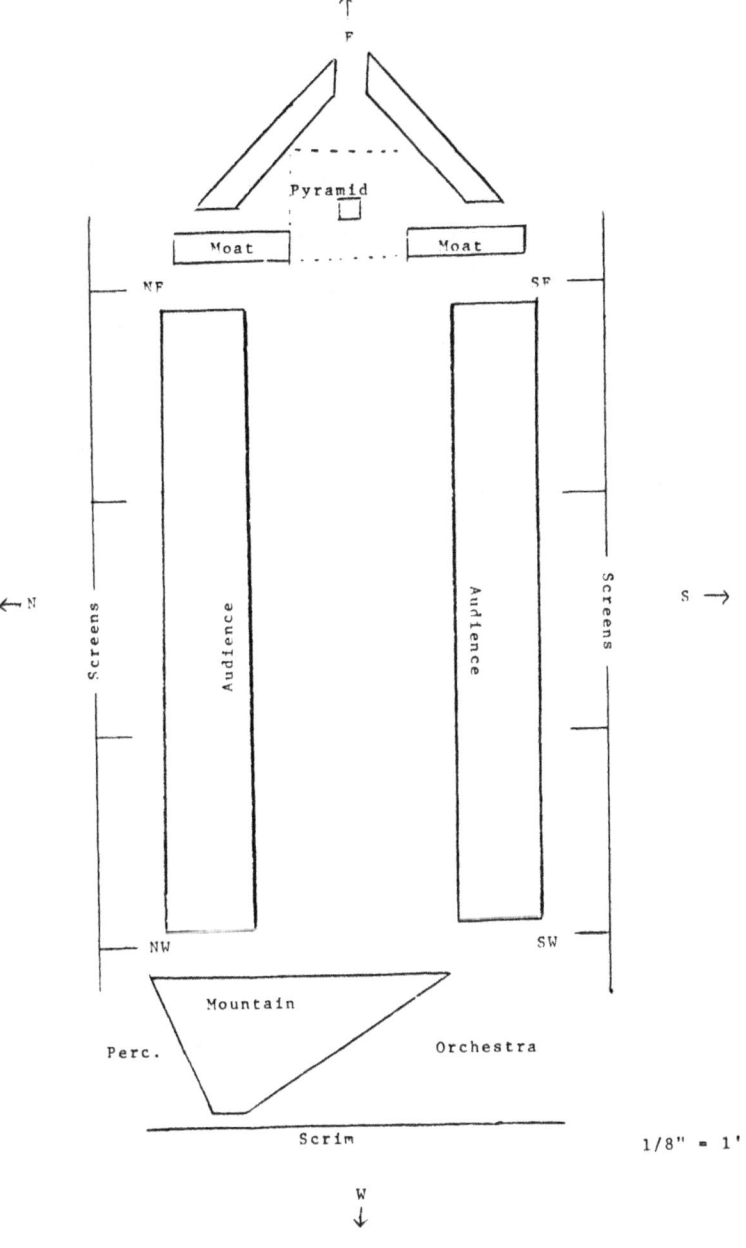

1/8" = 1'

69

For all enquiries regarding motion picture, television, and other media rights, please contact Samuel French.

MUSIC USE NOTE

Licensees are solely responsible for obtaining formal written permission from copyright owners to use copyrighted music in the performance of this play and are strongly cautioned to do so. If no such permission is obtained by the licensee, then the licensee must use only original music that the licensee owns and controls. Licensees are solely responsible and liable for all music clearances and shall indemnify the copyright owners of the play(s) and their licensing agent, Samuel French, against any costs, expenses, losses and liabilities arising from the use of music by licensees. Please contact the appropriate music licensing authority in your territory for the rights to any incidental music.

IMPORTANT BILLING AND CREDIT REQUIREMENTS

If you have obtained performance rights to this title, please refer to your licensing agreement for important billing and credit requirements.

www.ingramcontent.com/pod-product-compliance
Lightning Source LLC
Chambersburg PA
CBHW071930130726
47909CB00014B/2904